Franklin and the Bubble Gum

From an episode of the animated TV series *Franklin,*
produced by Nelvana Limited, Neurones France s.a.r.l. and
Neurones Luxembourg S.A, based on the Franklin books
by Paulette Bourgeois and Brenda Clark.

Story written by Sharon Jennings.

Illustrated by Sean Jeffrey, Sasha McIntyre and Jelena Sisic.

Based on the TV episode *Franklin's Candy Caper,* written by Bob Ardiel.

® Kids Can Read is a registered trademark of Kids Can Press Ltd.

Franklin

Franklin is a trademark of Kids Can Press Ltd.
The character of Franklin was created by Paulette Bourgeois and Brenda Clark.
Text © 2006 Contextx Inc.
Illustrations © 2006 Brenda Clark Illustrator Inc.

Kids Can Press acknowledges the financial support of the Government of Ontario,
through the Ontario Media Development Corporation's Ontario Book Initiative; the
Ontario Arts Council; the Canada Council for the Arts; and the Government of Canada,
through the BPIDP, for our publishing activity.

Published in Canada by
Kids Can Press Ltd.
29 Birch Avenue
Toronto, ON M4V 1E2

Published in the U.S. by
Kids Can Press Ltd.
2250 Military Road
Tonawanda, NY 14150

www.kidscanpress.com

Series editor: Tara Walker
Edited by Jennifer Stokes
Designed by Céleste Gagnon

Printed and bound in China

The hardcover edition of this book is smyth sewn casebound.
The paperback edition of this book is limp sewn with a drawn-on cover.

CM 06 0 9 8 7 6 5 4 3 2 1
CM PA 06 0 9 8 7 6 5 4 3 2 1

Library and Archives Canada Cataloguing in Publication

Jennings, Sharon
    Franklin and the bubble gum / Sharon Jennings ; illustrated by Sean
Jeffrey, Sasha McIntyre, Jelena Sisic.

(Kids Can read)
The character Franklin was created by Paulette Bourgeois and Brenda Clark.
ISBN-13: 978-1-55337-816-7 (bound).   ISBN-13: 978-1-55337-817-4 (pbk.)
ISBN-10: 1-55337-816-4 (bound).   ISBN-10: 1-55337-817-2 (pbk.)

I. Jeffrey, Sean II. McIntyre, Sasha III. Sisic, Jelena IV. Bourgeois, Paulette
V. Clark, Brenda VI. Title. VII. Series: Kids Can read (Toronto, Ont.)

PS8569.E563F714575 2006   jC813'.54   C2005-901586-1

Kids Can Press is a l☺rus™ Entertainment company

Franklin and the Bubble Gum

Kids Can Press

Franklin can tie his shoes.

Franklin can count by twos.

And Franklin can get into trouble.

Franklin doesn't want to get into trouble.

He doesn't mean to get into trouble.

But sometimes, trouble happens.

One day, Franklin saw a penny

on the sidewalk.

"Hmmm," said Franklin.

"Granny always says,

Find a penny, pick it up.

All the day you'll have good luck."

Franklin picked up the penny.

Then he ran to the candy store.

A new gum ball
machine stood
in front of
Mr. Mole's store.

Franklin put
in his penny.
He turned the handle.

A red gum ball
fell out.

A blue gum ball
fell out.

"Wow!" said Franklin.

He held his hat under the spout.

All the gum balls fell out.

"I did find a lucky penny!"

said Franklin.

Franklin ran to find his friends.

"Look!" he shouted.

"I found a lucky penny and look!"

Everyone looked.

"I got all the gum from Mr. Mole's

new gum ball machine!"

"Wow!" said everyone.

Franklin shared the gum balls
with his friends.

"I can chew five
gum balls at once,"
said Rabbit.

"I can chew ten,"
said Bear.

"I can blow the
biggest bubble,"
said Franklin.

Franklin blew a giant bubble.

POP!

"I love bubble gum," said Franklin.

Just then, Beaver rode into the park.

"Guess what!" she shouted.

"Mr. Mole's been robbed!"

"That's terrible!" said Franklin.

"Someone took all Mr. Mole's

bubble gum," said Beaver.

"That's terrible!" said Franklin again.

"Who would ..."

Franklin stopped talking.

Everyone turned to look at Franklin.

"Uh-oh," said Franklin.

"Wait a minute,"

said Beaver.

"Why are all of

you chewing gum?"

"Franklin gave it

to us," said Bear.

Franklin told Beaver

about the lucky penny.

"There is no such thing as

a lucky penny," said Beaver.

"Well, it sure wasn't a lucky penny

for Mr. Mole," agreed Franklin.

Franklin sat down to think.

"I have to give Mr. Mole

his gum back," he said.

"But it's chewed!" said Beaver.

Franklin did some more thinking.

"I know!" he said.

"I'll pay Mr. Mole for the gum."

Everyone ran to Franklin's house.

Franklin grabbed his piggy bank.

He shook out all his pennies.

"Let's go!" he said.

Everyone ran to the candy store.

The gum ball machine was still empty.

Franklin put a penny in the slot.

He turned the handle.

He put another penny in the slot.

He turned the handle again.

"Hurry up!" said Beaver.

Franklin put the last penny in the slot.

No one saw Mr. Mole come outside.

"Wait!" said Mr. Mole.

"Don't put a penny

into an empty machine."

Mr. Mole unlocked the lid.

He poured in a bag of gum balls.

"Someone stole all my gum

this morning," said Mr. Mole.

Everyone looked at Franklin.

Franklin looked
up at the sky.

He looked down
at the ground.

He jiggled from foot to foot.

Finally, Franklin said, "Well, Mr. Mole ...

You see, Mr. Mole ..."

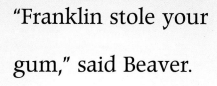

"Franklin stole your
gum," said Beaver.

"I didn't!" said Franklin.

"Well, I did, but I didn't *want* to.

I didn't *mean* to. I had a lucky penny,

and all your gum fell out."

"And Franklin paid you back," said Bear.

"He just put all his pennies

in your gum ball machine."

"Hmmm," said Mr. Mole.

Mr. Mole put a penny

in the gum ball machine.

He turned the handle.

A red gum ball

fell out.

A blue gum ball

fell out.

"Uh-oh!" said Franklin.

He grabbed his hat.

All the gum balls fell out.

"Hmph!" said Mr. Mole.

"This machine

is broken."

"See, Franklin?" said Beaver.

"I told you there's

no such thing as

a lucky penny."

"Am I in trouble?"

asked Franklin.

"No," said Mr. Mole. "You were

very honest about an honest mistake."

Franklin nodded.

"So thank you," said Mr. Mole.

"You may keep all the

bubble gum."

"I love bubble gum!" said Franklin.

"See, Beaver?" said Franklin. "I told you it was a lucky penny!"